GROVER AND BIG BIRD'S PASSOVER CELEBRATION

Tilda Balsley and Ellen Fischer

Illustrated by Tom Leigh

KAR-BEN
PUBLISHING

For my nephew Walter and his sweet family – T.B

Dedicated with love to Jeanne, Liz and Scott – E.L.F.

For Sarah – T.L.

KAR-BEN PUBLISHING
A division of Lerner Publishing Group, Inc.
241 First Avenue North
Minneapolis, MN 55401 USA
1-800-4-Karben

Website address: www.karben.com

Library of Congress Cataloging-in-Publication Data

Balsley, Tilda.
    Grover and Big Bird's Passover celebration / by Tilda Balsley and Ellen Fischer ; illustrated by Tom Leigh.
        p.   cm.
    Summary: While making their way to Brosh's house for the Passover seder, Grover and Big Bird talk about the history and traditions of the holiday, and find opportunities to do good deeds.
    ISBN 978-0-7613-8491-5 (lib. bdg. : alk. paper)
    ISBN 978-1-4677-0995-8 (EB pdf)
    [1. Judaism—Customs and practices—Fiction. 2. Passover—Fiction. 3. Seder—Fiction.]
I. Fischer, Ellen, 1947- II. Leigh, Tom, ill. III. Title.
PZ7.B21385Gro 2013
[E]—dc23   2012009496

Manufactured in the United States of America
3-43144-12449-11/2/2016

HELLO EVERYBODEEE!

It is I, your furry blue friend Grover, writing from Israel. I am going to tell you about all the adventures that Big Bird and yours truly had on the way to the seder at Brosh's house and all of the mitzvot (good deeds) we did. A seder is a special Passover meal where Jewish families tell the story of the Exodus from Egypt, sing songs, say prayers, and eat delicious foods.

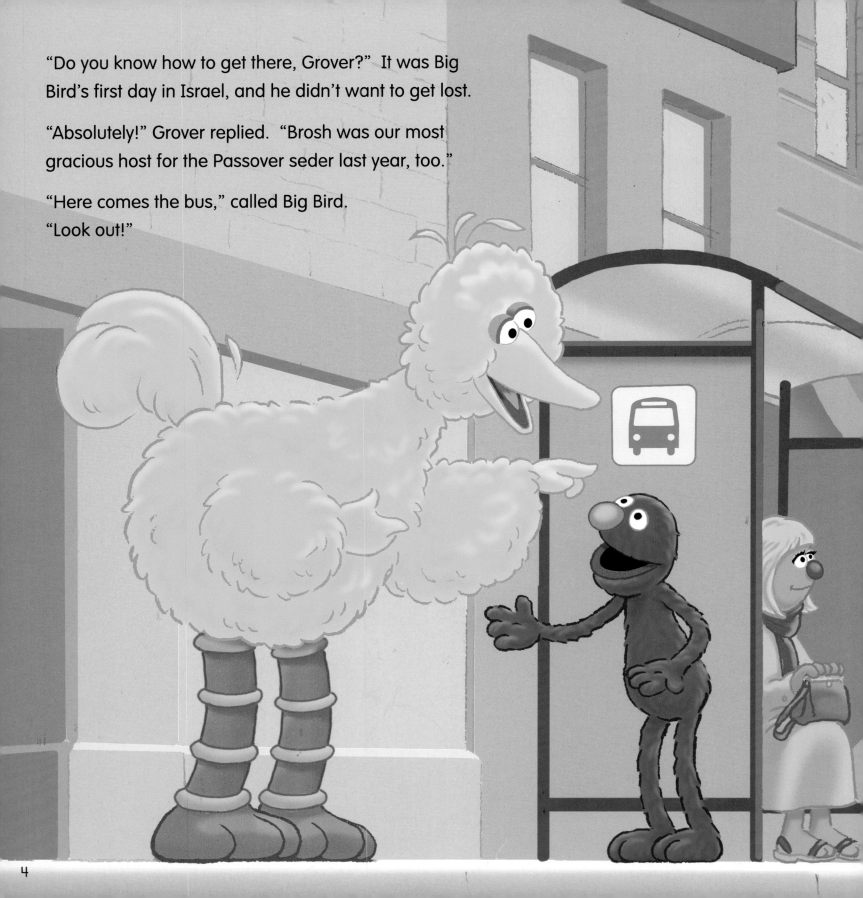

"Do you know how to get there, Grover?" It was Big Bird's first day in Israel, and he didn't want to get lost.

"Absolutely!" Grover replied. "Brosh was our most gracious host for the Passover seder last year, too."

"Here comes the bus," called Big Bird. "Look out!"

"Boker tov," Grover said to the bus driver. "That is 'good morning' in Hebrew, Big Bird."

"I hope we'll get there early enough to help," said Big Bird. "I love to help."

"Do not worry," said Grover. "We have plenty of time."

Bumpity bump bump. The bus came to a stop. "Flat tire," said the driver. "Everybody off. Another bus will be along shortly."

Big Bird and Grover sat on a bench, waiting.

"Look, Grover." Big Bird pointed to a puppy running past them, his leash dangling. A little boy was racing after him.

"Farfel! Oh, Farfel!" he cried.

Big Bird jumped up and ran. He caught up with the dog, and stepped on the leash to stop him.

"Excellent!" said Grover, patting the puppy.

Big Bird patted the puppy, too, and handed the leash to the boy. "Bye-bye."

"And bye-bye to our bus, too," said Grover. "But *no problemo*. We can take a shortcut through the park to the next bus stop."

"Hey, Grover!" said Big Bird. "Come smell these beautiful flowers. But watch out for the sticker bush!"

"Too late. I am stuck."

"Hang on, Grover," Big Bird called. "I'm coming." Snip snip snip. Big Bird used his beak to unstick his friend.

8

"That was totally awesome, Big Bird," said Grover. "You set me free.
Did you know that the holiday of Passover is all about freedom?"

Big Bird shook his head, "Freedom for furry blue monsters?"

"No, Big Bird. Freedom from mean old Pharaoh. A long time ago, the Jewish
people were slaves in Egypt. A man named Moses led them to freedom."

As they walked, Grover thought about Brosh and Avigail getting ready for the seder. "I bet Avigail is practicing the Four Questions right this very minute."

Big Bird scratched his head. "Is one of the questions 'Where are my friends Grover and Big Bird?'"

"That is very funny, Big Bird. But the Four Questions are part of the seder. I remember the beginning: 'Why is this night different from all other nights?'"

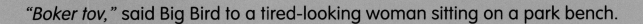

"*Boker tov,*" said Big Bird to a tired-looking woman sitting on a park bench.

She nodded and moved her bags over to make room for them. "I'm just resting a minute," she said. "I had so many things to buy for my seder."

Grover peeked in the bags. "You are not kidding! Matzah, horseradish, eggs, parsley, salt, a roasted bone, apples, and nuts. Please allow this furry blue monster to carry your groceries."

"And this big yellow bird," added Big Bird.

When they got to her house, the woman took the groceries.
"Todah rabah," she thanked them. *"Shalom."*

Grover waved. *"Shalom* is the Hebrew word for 'good-bye,'" he told
Big Bird. "But shalom also means 'hello' and 'peace.'"

"Wow!" said Big Bird. "That's a lot of work for one little word."

"You said it," Grover agreed. "Is it not fascinating?"

"Yes, but now we'd really better hurry," said Big Bird.

"Did you know," said Grover, "that the Jewish people were in a hurry when they followed Moses out of Egypt? They could not even wait for their bread to rise. That is why we eat flat, crunchy matzah on Passover."

Grover looked around. "It is definitely time to go, but I am a bit confused. Where are we exactly?" Then he saw a tumbledown truck turn down the street.

"Moishe Oofnik!" cried Grover. "We are so happy to see you."

"Happy?" repeated Moishe. "Yuck!"

"What Grover means," explained Big Bird, "is that we're lost and we don't want to be late for Brosh's seder. Can you help us?"

"Help?" repeated Moishe. "Oofniks don't help!"

Grover had to think fast. "There will be lots of bitter herbs at dinner."

"Why didn't you say so?" said Moishe. "My favorite! Hop in."

Brosh opened the door. "Big Bird! Grover! And Moishe!"

"Without Moishe, we would not be here," said Grover.

"What took you so long?" asked Avigail.

"One exciting adventure after another," answered Big Bird. "A bus with a flat tire started it all. Then we rescued a puppy on the loose, we helped a woman with her groceries . . ."

"And do not forget, Big Bird," said Grover, "you set me free from that sticker bush."

"Well," said Brosh, "we're glad you're here now, and we have an extra chair for Moishe."

Avigail whispered, "Isn't that for Elijah the Prophet?"

Brosh laughed. "You're right, Avigail. But we'll bring in another chair for Moishe."

19

Avigail asked the Four Questions, and everyone took turns reading the stories and blessings from the Haggadah. They sang *Dayenu* and ate the delicious Passover foods.

Moishe had three helpings of bitter herbs. "I love this stuff!" he exclaimed, his eyes watering.

And Big Bird surprised everyone by finding the afikomen.

Before the night was over, Avigail begged Grover to retell the story of the day's adventures.

". . . And that is why," Grover finished, "we were absolutely no help at all in preparing this beautiful seder meal."

"But Grover," said Brosh, "while we were getting ready for the seder, you spent your day doing *mitzvot*—good deeds. That's a very important kind of helping."

"Whew!" said Big Bird. "My brain is full of new words, my heart is full with new friends, and my tummy is full of matzah. Can I come for seder next year?"

Brosh smiled. "Of course! As the Haggadah says, 'Next year in Jerusalem!'"

About Passover

Passover is a week-long holiday in the spring when Jews celebrate the biblical Exodus of the Jewish people from slavery in Egypt. The holiday begins with a festive meal called a seder. Symbolic foods at the seder recall the bitterness of slavery, the haste in which the Jews left, and the joy of freedom. During the holiday week no *hametz* (leavened food, such as bread) is eaten. Matzah, a special flat cracker, takes the place of bread.

About the Authors and Illustrator

Tilda Balsley has written many books for Kar-Ben, bringing her stories to life with rhyme, rhythm, and humor. Now that *Sesame Street* characters populate her stories, she says writing has never been more fun. Tilda lives with her husband and their rescue Shih Tzu in Reidsville, North Carolina.

Ellen Fischer, not blue and furry, or as cute and loveable as Grover, was born in St. Louis. Following graduation from Washington University, she taught children with special needs, then ESL (English as a Second Language) at a Jewish Day School. She lives in Greensboro, North Carolina, with her husband. They have three children.

Tom Leigh is a children's book author and longtime illustrator of *Sesame Street* and Muppet books. He lives on Little Deer Isle off the coast of Maine with his four dogs and two cats.

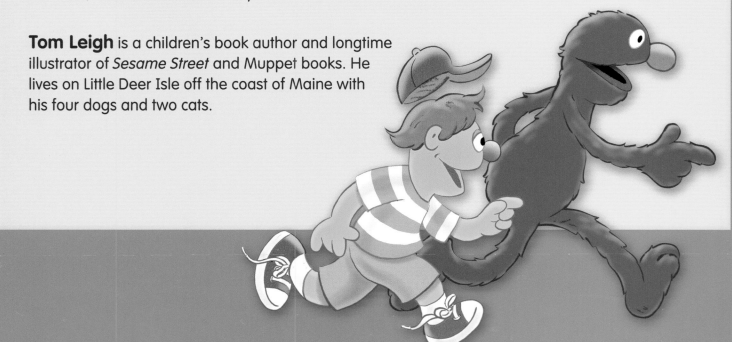